The Way to the Zoo

For Sylvie, who always puts you through

First U.S. edition 2014

Library of Congress Catalog Card Number 2013952847
ISBN 978-0-7636-7317-8

14 15 16 17 18 19 CCP 10 9 8 7 6 5 4 3 2 1

Printed in Shenzhen, Guangdong, China

This book was typeset in URW Egyptienne T.
The illustrations were done in pen, pencil pastel, and watercolor.

Candlewick Press
99 Dover Street
Somerville, Massachusetts 02144

visit us at www.candlewick.com

The Way to the Zoo

JOHN BURNINGHAM

CANDLEWICK PRESS

One evening, just before Sylvie went to sleep, she thought she could see a door in the wall of her bedroom.

She decided to look again in the morning to see if the door was really there.

In the morning, Sylvie was late for school
and forgot about the door until bedtime.

When Sylvie was ready for bed,
she found the door and managed to open it.
She could see some steps going down,
and beyond them was a passageway.

Sylvie found a flashlight and went down
the steps and along the passageway
for a while, wondering where it would go.

In the distance, she could see what seemed
to be another door.

This door was heavy, but Sylvie used
all her strength and at last it opened.

She found herself in the zoo, with lots
of animals looking at her.

It was getting late. Sylvie had to get back to her room and go to sleep because she had school again in the morning.

Sylvie asked a little bear to come back with her. He did and slept in her bed.

She made sure the bear was back in the zoo and the door in the wall was closed before she left for school.

The next few nights, all the animals wanted to come
to Sylvie's room, but she could only take the smaller ones.

One night she brought the penguins back,

but they made a big mess splashing in the bathroom.

Then she came back with a tiger and her cub.

The tiger slept in a chair, and her cub slept in Sylvie's bed.

Another night Sylvie let the birds come.

Sylvie had to ask some animals to go back to the zoo because they stole things . . .

or were too smelly to have in her room.

The baby elephant burst into tears
because it was too big for the passageway.

A baby rhino was able to get through the passageway,
but Sylvie did not want the rhino in her bed.

So she covered it in towels
for the night.

One morning Sylvie woke up very late
and had to rush to get ready for school.

When she came home later that day, she knew something was wrong. There were noises coming from the living room.

She had forgotten to close the door in her bedroom wall.

The living room was full of animals.

Sylvie got very upset,
and all the animals left.

Sylvie's mother would be home soon,
so she had very little time to clean up.

Sylvie hadn't quite finished when her mother arrived.

"Oh Sylvie, Sylvie," her mother said. "All I have to do is leave you at home when I go out for a while and it looks as if you had the whole zoo in here!"

Sylvie still sometimes has animals visit
at night, perhaps a baby bear or something
else small and furry.

But she always makes sure that the way
to the zoo is closed before she goes to school.